—105—
PUBLISHING
EST. 2020

Introduction:

Come with me on this *Born To Win* journey!

This book was inspired by my grandchildren Bella Wallace and Eliana Bray. I want them to know at an early age who they are and what gift they have to offer to the world. I want them to know that the sky isn't even the limit, and you can do and become anything you put your mind to.

In this book, I highlight some of the GREATS from A-to-Z, past and present, who didn't have it easy at all but still overcame to walk in their purpose. Parents, I encourage you to read this book with your children, as it identifies purpose and destiny. Encourage our children to stay focused and don't take "no" for an answer. Failure is not the end, quitting is.

Born To Win

By: Sherika Bray
Cover by: Ananta Mohanta
Interior Illustrations by: Amy Marques

Start where you are, use what you have, and do what you can.

A is for Arthur Ashe:
- American Tennis Player
- First black player selected in the United States to Davis Cup Team

Change will not come if we wait for some other person.

B is for Barak Obama:
- 44th American president
- First African American President

Being beautiful is all in the attitude, it's about confidence.

C is for Ciara:
- Professional American singer, song writer, dancer, model, & actress
- One Grammy
- Generated 8 billboard hot 100 top 10 singles
- 3 MTV music video awards

Do what you have to, to do what you want to.

D is for Denzel Washington:
- American actor, director, and producer
- Known for his performances on screen and on stage

Many people know how to criticize but few know how to praise.

E is for Ethel Waters:
- Blues singer in the 1920's
- First African American to star in her own Tv show "1939"
- Nominated for her first Emmy in 1962

Tough times don't last long, tough people do.

F is for Floyd Mayweather:
- American professional Boxer
- Professional boxing promoter
- One of the greatest boxers of all time
- Net worth of $450 million

If you don't have anything to say, your photographs aren't going to say much.

G is for Gordan Parks:
- American photographer, musician, writer and film director
- Prominent in the 1940's - 1970's

Slavery is the next thing to hell.

H is for Harriet Tubman:
- American abolitionist & political activist
- Founder of the underground railroad
- Made 13 missions to rescue approximately 70 enslaved people

A child of the sun, black is my contenance, yet I stand before you in the light of my soul.

I is for Ira Aldridge:

- First African American Actor to achieve success on the international stage

A life is not important except in the impact it has on other lives.

J is for Jackie Robinson:
- American professional baseball player
- First African American to play in major league baseball in the modern era
- Broke the baseball color line when he started at first base for the Brooklyn Dodgers April 15th, 1947

Children who are treated like they are uneducable, almost invariably become uneducable.

K is for Kenneth Clark:

• Psychologist & Professor

Failure will never overtake me if my determination to succeed is strong enough.

L is for Lynette Woodard:
- American basketball and Hall of Fame player
- Former head women's basketball coach at Winthrop University

To ignore evil is to become accomplice to it.

M is for Martin Luther King Jr:
- American minister & activist
- Most visible spokesman & leader in the American Civil Rights Movement from 1955 until his assassnation in 1968

Anger is a manifestation of a deeper issue.

N is for Naomi Campbell:
- British model, actress, singer & businesswoman
- She Began her career at the age of 15 and established herself amongst the most recognizable

Surround yourself with people who are going to take you higher.

O is for Oprah Winfrey:
- American talk show host, television producer, actress, author & philanthropist
- Net worth 2.6 billion dollars

Imagination who can sing thy force or who describes the swiftness of thy course.

P is for Phillis Wheatley:
- Spent most of her life enslaved
- Never received formal education
- First African American & third woman to publish a book of poems

Ego is just an overdressed insecurity.

Q is for Quincy Jones:
- American record producer, musician, songwriter, composer, arranger, film, & television producer
- 70 years in entertainment
- 80 Grammy nominations, 28 Grammys, & Grammy Legend Award winner in 1992

I didn't accept it, I received it.

R is for Richard Allen:
- Minister, educator, & writer
- One of the most active & influential leaders
- Founder of the African Methodist Episcopal Church - the first black denomination in United States

Truth is all powerful and will prevail.

S is for Sojourner Truth:
- Women's right activist
- Born into slavery but escaped with her infant daughter to freedom in 1826
- Went to court to recover her son & won
- First black woman to win a case against the white man

Developing a good work ethic is key.

T is for Tyler Perry:
- American actor, director, producer, & screenwriter
- In 2011 he was listed in Forbes as the highest paid man in the entertainment business earning $130 million
- He created & performed the Madea character

Inadequate education in childhood and race discrimination gave me strength.

U is for Ulysses Gooch:
- One of the first inductees to the Black Aviation Hall of Fame
- American Entrepreneur
- Aviation Entrepreneur
- Kansas Politician

All dreams are within reach all you have to do is keep moving towards them.

V is for Viola Davis:
- Youngest and first African American to achieve the triple crown of acting
- American actress & producer

Work is the thing that happens around game time.

W is for Wayne Brady:
• American television personality, comedian, actor, & singer

When you go to work you want to have fun because when you're having fun you are not really working.

X is for Xavier Woods:
- American professional Wrestler
- Winner of the 2021 King of the Ring tournament

No matter how hard it gets never give up; always believe.

Y is for Yolanda Adams:
- American Gospel singer
- Host of her own nationally syndicated morning show
- Sold nearly 10 million albums worldwide with some albums achieving multi-platinum status

If you are silent about your pain, they'll kill you and say you enjoyed it.

Z is for Zora Neale Hurston:
- American Author, anthropologist, & filmmaker
- The most popular of her four novels is, *Their Eyes Were Watching God* published in 1937

105 Publishing LLC
Austin, TX
ww.105publishing.com

Made in the USA
Coppell, TX
28 July 2022

80564223R00019